I love you, Daddy

This book belongs to

_____

_____

Written by Jillian Harker
Illustrated by Kristina Stephenson

This edition published by Parragon in 2011

Parragon
Queen Street House
4 Queen Street
Bath BA1 1HE, UK

ISBN 978-1-4454-5553-2

Printed in China

I love you, Daddy

Bath • New York • Singapore • Hong Kong • Cologne • Delhi
Melbourne • Amsterdam • Johannesburg • Auckland • Shenzhen

"You're growing tall, Little Bear," said Daddy
Bear. "Big enough to come climbing with me."
Little Bear's eyes opened wide in surprise.
"Do you really mean that?"
Daddy Bear nodded. He led Little Bear to
a giant tree.

And, suddenly, Little Bear found he could. "I love Daddy," thought Little Bear.

"You're growing brave, Little Bear,"
said Daddy Bear. "Daring enough
to collect honey with me."
Little Bear gasped.
"Could I really?"
Daddy Bear winked.
He led Little Bear to
another tree and pointed
to a hole in the trunk.

Little Bear reached out his paw.
A furious buzzing filled his ears.
Little Bear pulled his paw back.

"Just be quick," Daddy Bear said. "You have thick fur. The bees can't hurt you. You can do it!" he smiled.

"You're growing clever, Little Bear.
Smart enough to find a good winter den."
Little Bear grinned.
"Do you really think so?"
"I know so," said Daddy Bear.

"Just be quick," Daddy Bear said. "You have thick fur. The bees can't hurt you. You can do it!" he smiled.

And, suddenly, Little Bear found he could.

"I love Daddy," thought Little Bear.

"You're growing clever, Little Bear.
Smart enough to find a good winter den."
Little Bear grinned.
"Do you really think so?"
"I know so," said Daddy Bear.

Little Bear set off.

"Not too far from food," said Daddy Bear.

"Ready for when spring comes."

Little Bear sniffed the wind.

"Look for high ground,"
said Daddy Bear,
"to keep us dry."
Little Bear padded up
over the rocks.

"Somewhere safe and warm,"
said Daddy Bear, "away
from danger."

"Here!" called Little Bear as he disappeared into a deep cave.

Daddy Bear followed. He looked all around.
"Perfect!" he said.
"I love Daddy," thought Little Bear.

"Did I climb well?" Little Bear asked,
on the way home.

"You did!" replied Daddy Bear.

"Was I brave?" asked Little Bear.

"You were!" answered Daddy Bear.

"Did I find a good den?" asked Little Bear.

"The very best!" smiled Daddy Bear.

"I'm proud of you, Little Bear."

Soon, Little Bear and Daddy Bear reached home.
And, suddenly, Little Bear felt very tired,
but there was something he wanted to say.

"I love you, D..." began Little Bear.
But he didn't finish.

Daddy Bear stroked Little Bear's head.
"I love you, too," he said.

"Goodnight, Little Bear."